W. T. Currie BA

Brodie's Notes on Mark Twain's

Huckleberry Finn

Pan Educational London and Sydney

First published 1977 by Pan Books Ltd,
Cavaye Place, London sw10 9pg
2   3   4   5   6   7   8   9
© W. T. Currie 1977
ISBN 0 330 50058 9
Printed and bound in Great Britain by
Richard Clay (The Chaucer Press) Ltd,
Bungay, Suffolk

Contents

The author v

The book 1
Approach and structure 1

Themes and people 4
Autobiography 4
The Mississippi 5
Slavery and freedom 6
Folklore and superstition 8

The characters 9

Notes 15

Revision questions 36

The author

Mark Twain is the pseudonym of Samuel Langhorne Clemens (1835–1910). He adopted his pen-name from a well-known call of the man sounding the river in shallow places ('mark twain' meaning 'by the mark two fathoms').

His hometown of Hannibal is almost in the geographical centre of America and has the wide Mississippi to the East. This river, some 2,470 miles long, he later called his University. He was to say:

When I find a well-drawn character in fiction or biography I generally take a warm personal interest in him for the reason that I have known him before – met him on the river.

Just as Geoffrey Chaucer used in his *Canterbury Tales* the characters who entered the gates of London from all over the world, so did Mark Twain turn to account the vast concourse of riverborne life.

Mark's father passed on his own optimism to the boy. The family lived on the verge of great things, buoyed with visions of vast wealth. Always there were high hopes of soaring land values. The rather slack and casual society that surrounded him deprived him of regular schooling and any firm hope of this vanished with his father's death in 1847.

At twelve, therefore, he found himself apprenticed to a printer and, restless by nature, he took to the road with his craft.

In 1856 he set off down the river, ostensibly as the start of a voyage to South America. Before the steamer had gone very far he apprenticed himself to Horace Bixby, the boat's pilot. It was thus that in 1859 he achieved his boyhood ambition and became a Licensed Pilot on the Mississippi. In 1861, however, the advent of the American Civil War brought trade on the river to a standstill and Clemens departed for the west. In Nevada he worked as secretary to his brother, who was in the service of the governor, and while there tried gold-mining without success.

He soon turned to journalism and the day-to-day change of assignment suited his nature perfectly. This had a profound effect on his style which was also influenced by the lectures he gave on his extensive travels.

In 1867 his first real story, *The Celebrated Jumping Frog of Calaveros County*, alerted his readers to the fact that here was a new humorous writer. In the same year he set out to visit France, Italy and Palestine, gathering material for his first book, *Innocents Abroad*, published in 1869. The story sold 150,000 copies and Mark Twain was firmly established as a humorist.

Marriage in 1870 to the wealthy Olivia Langdon followed, and even he was surprised at finding himself accepted into her well-to-do family. Some critics suggest that thereafter both he and his style became cramped as a result of this union, but letters to the lady in question seem to be loving enough to leave this matter open. Whatever the truth may be, he certainly looked back on his boyhood days with real nostalgia. In 1876 *The Adventures of Tom Sawyer*, describing the lawless side of vagrant boyhood, appeared.

In the Preface to the book the author says that most of the adventures recorded really occurred and 'one or two were experiences of my own, the rest those of schoolmates of mine'.

He goes on to say:

Huck Finn is drawn from life; Tom Sawyer also, but not from an individual; he is a combination of the characteristics of three boys whom I knew, and therefore belongs to the composite order of architecture.

There is no doubt that one of the three boys was the author himself.

In 1883 *Life on the Mississippi* was published; a full and vivid narrative of the scenes he loved best. This river ran through his life and he knew more about it than about anything else. He had learned about it at a time when his perceptions and memory were at their sharpest. The Mississippi had imposed its own discipline on him and he had learned its ways 'in the midst of actual events and under the pressures of serious responsibilities'.

Mark Twain had once written:

Part of my plan has been to try to remind adults of what they once were themselves, and of how they felt and thought and talked, and what queer enterprises they sometimes engaged in.

This he put to the test with the publication in 1884 of *The Adventures of Huckleberry Finn*. Here, through the eyes of a much more sharply realized Huck than we find in *Tom Sawyer*, he gives us the full richness of American life on the Mississippi at that time. Mingled with this dramatic account there are the author's own reflections on life in general. Here, as in Chaucer, we find a relish for all phases of comedy and the foibles of human beings.

Academic recognition followed and in 1888 he was created an honorary MA of Yale University. What he most valued, however, was the degree of Doctor of Literature conferred on him by the Convocation of Oxford University in 1907.

In the two novels of boyhood he exhausted his vein of reminiscence, or perhaps lost the interest in it which could fully arouse his imagination.

When he died, in 1910, he could perhaps have had wry satisfaction that his death caused a more universal regret than had ever followed the death of any other American man of letters.

The book

Approach and structure

The greatest charm about this book is that it can be read at
different levels of awareness, and it can be re-read at intervals
with growing understanding.

For Americans its great achievement is that it broke away
from European culture both in content and in language.
Lionel Trilling, in fact, calls it 'one of the central documents
of American culture'. Rarely has any book succeeded in sus-
taining the use of colloquial speech throughout with such
success. Mark Twain himself calls our attention to the number
of dialects he has used, and tells us that he has taken great
pains to ensure that the shadings have not been done hap-
hazardly. Perhaps our ears are not so closely attuned to
spoken American as Twain's original readers, but it is a
remarkable achievement that once we have made the initial
effort we scarcely notice the dialect at all. This is something
akin to the ideal way of reading Shakespeare, without even
noticing or being held back by Elizabethan usage.

Taking such facts into consideration it is still remarkable
that a book which was called:

'vulgar, rough, inelegant, irreverent, coarse, semi-obscene,
 trashy and vicious'

should be considered a serious contender for literary honours.
Indeed, when *Huckleberry Finn* was banned from the children's
room of certain American libraries Twain reacted in typically
facetious fashion. In a letter to one librarian he said: 'I wrote
Tom Sawyer and *Huckleberry Finn* for adults exclusively, and it
always distresses me when I find that boys and girls have been
allowed access to them.' We may only hope that the Brooklyn

librarian realized that the letter had been written tongue firmly in cheek.

To most people, however, it is Huckleberry Finn's casual approach to language and ownership of property for example, that appeals to us. His basic badness is rarely sinful, simply boyish. There is nothing vicious about him and we envy his ability to throw off the trammels and restraints of society. Indeed, we regret that he has to be troubled by conscience at all. In a way this is a great novel of escape and, when he wrote it, Mark Twain obviously had a certain amount of nostalgia for the days of freedom that he had enjoyed as a boy. Days marked by adventure that was not too dangerous, and by unrestraint that was not too harmful.

In order to try to remind his adult readers of what they once were, Mark Twain has written this picaresque tale; one in which the adventures of an engagingly roguish hero are described in a series of usually humorous or satiric episodes that frequently depict in realistic detail the everyday life of the common people. Cervantes had done this in *Don Quixote* and Kipling pictured a full sub-continent with his descriptions of the hills and plains of India in *Kim*. In each of these also we follow the quest of the hero to an ultimate goal.

Holding the whole tale together is, of course, the River. The Mississippi was ideal for Twain's purposes. He knew it intimately and it had formed part of his childhood and conditioned his growing up. The folk who lived on its banks were vastly interesting to him and they were of all varieties of mankind. They were there to enjoy and to be enjoyed. This exciting kaleidoscopic world was indeed an epitome of the United States of that time. In fact the whole of his early life, spent close to the river and under its influence, was a time when he was gathering material about people and places that he was to use to full effect later. This was to be indeed, 'American life formed into great fiction'.

Twain, of course, is a great humorist with a full delight in life in general and in all phases of comedy. He was determined to please, and if at times he strives to do this too elaborately we may credit him with an honest intention. Throughout his life a joke told at his own expense was twice as good as one told about somebody else. His aim is to pass on these jokes and topical allusions to us, his readers. If they sometimes appear trivial, again, it is almost as though in their sheer weight and number we must find something to our taste. The author wishes nothing other than to entertain us: no bad intention when we come to consider it.

The first release of creative energy in 1876 took him up to Chapter 16, and beyond this point he could not go. Cairo and Jim's freedom seemed as far away as at the beginning of the story and Twain abandoned the manuscript, even threatening to burn it. It is almost as though the only happiness the pair is going to find is on the raft, away from the rest of mankind. It is this theme that the author was to develop in the next seven years before he could finish the story. This is the contrast between the freedom they had so far enjoyed on the river and the predominantly unattractive life of the towns. Here he brings to bear all his deep feeling for nature and natural surroundings in an almost mystical climate, where we can only wonder at man's inhumanity to his fellow creatures.

Episode follows episode as Huck and Jim drift at the will of the river towards their ultimate goal, the freedom of the Negro. It would not be straining analogy too far to see something like the progress of John Bunyan's Pilgrim through the dangers and difficulties of life, in the theme of the river journey of these two American pilgrims. They, too, meet with danger and adversity on their voyage, and the digressions they take from the main way add much to the total meaning of their quest; indeed, the stories told in the frequent digressions are often more absorbing than the ostensible tale itself. So, at one level we have a stirring account of a dangerous journey and, just below the surface, the biting satire of the reformer. In the one case we can simply enjoy the story and in the other experience a slight feeling of unease as though Mark Twain has perpetrated his greatest practical joke by taking us in.

It is this dual purpose that should keep us alert as we read this novel, and it is clear evidence of the mastery of the author that we are forced to think about some major issues of life as we are lost in a seemingly simple tale of boyhood adventure.

Themes and people

Autobiography

It is a mistake to take the novel as too blatantly auto-biographical, although there are many people and scenes that Mark Twain had encountered in real life in the book. In his actual Autobiography the author makes it clear that he had definite people in mind as he was writing. Of Huckleberry Finn he says: 'I have drawn Tom Blankenship (Huck) exactly as he was. He was ignorant, unwashed, insufficiently fed; but he had as good a heart as ever any boy had.'

Later he gives a clue to the purpose of the book as he again discusses Huck: 'He was the only really independent person – boy or man – in the community, and by consequence he was tranquilly and continuously happy, and was envied by all the rest of us.'

We too envy the independence that the author writes of, and whatever our moral standpoint, have a sneaking regard for such a fortunate creature.

Sam Clemens of Hannibal, as we have said, stored his brain with the sights and sounds of his youth and brought them to the front of his mind when he needed them. For example, as a boy he had witnessed the first premeditated murder in his home town. The shooting of Boggs in our story actually happened on 24 January 1845, when a storekeeper, William Owsley, shot and killed Uncle Sam Smarr, described as: 'an honest man, but when drinking, a little turbulent'. The latter had provoked Owsley by claiming that he had cheated over money matters until the storekeeper could take no more and shot him. Out of this incident, held fast in memory, Mark Twain makes a graphic chapter and an equally gripping sequel when we watch Colonel Sherburn facing the wavering crowd who are not sure enough of themselves to carry through his lynching. It is of interest to note that the real Bill Owsley was not brought to trial till a year after the shooting and then acquitted on a plea of provocation by Sam Smarr. Owsley, however, was forced to leave the area as feeling had turned against him.

Revival meetings with their passionate preaching and dramatic conversions were all part of his childhood and troupes of itinerant players offered their repertory to the citizens of Hannibal. *The Royal Nonesuch* grew out of such events in his youth, though it probably stemmed also from the more robust oral tradition of the western frontier. Everything was grist to his mill and, through his genius, he transmuted it to pure gold.

The Mississippi

The river carries us along as it does Huck and Jim on their raft. There is something inexorable about it as we are borne gently along its slower reaches or rushed headlong as it runs in spate. It becomes more like the river of life as we realize that there is no turning back; there are rivulets that we do not want to pursue and stretches that we are unable to cover a second time. It is as though the author has left the threads of his adventure deliberately untied. Behind us life goes on and before us lies the unknown.

The Mississippi too is a symbol of the freedom that Huck seeks and it gives rise to some of the most poetic of the nature descriptions in the book. The early paragraphs of Chapter 19 show us clearly the deep effect the river had on Mark Twain's thinking. Everything about it appealed to him but, perhaps, particularly the feeling of isolation and loneliness: 'And afterwards we would watch the lonesomeness of the river, and kind of lazy along, and by-and-by lazy off to sleep.'

And as he says later: 'Sometimes we'd have that whole river to ourselves for the longest time.'

As well as the atmosphere of the river the author strives to give us some feeling of its size: 'It was a monstrous big river down there – sometimes a mile and a half wide.'

Right at the end of the book, when explanations are coming thick and fast, he makes Aunt Polly say:

'I might have expected it, letting him go off that way without anybody to watch him. So now I got to go and traipse all the way down the river, eleven hundred mile, and find out what that creetur's up to, *this* time; as long as I couldn't seem to get any answer out of you about it.'

It is from such passages that we begin to realize the scale of the book and the size of the canvas that the author has taken for his task of giving us what is almost a social history of his time.

Slavery and freedom

As a boy Mark Twain had spent many happy hours at the farm of John Quarles, his mother's brother. There he was to meet the prototype of Jim, the runaway slave. He says of the farm and of Uncle Dan'l: 'It was on the farm that I got my strong liking for his race, and my appreciation of certain of its fine qualities.'

Yet, through the voice of Huck Finn, the author was to express his guilt about such feelings towards a coloured man. Time and again the boy is haunted by the consequences of his aiding an escaped slave: 'People would call me a low-down Abolitionist and despise me for keeping mum.'

He is able to console himself with the fact that: 'I ain't going back there anyway,' so that he will not have to face the accusing friends of Hannibal. Indeed perhaps the most powerful passage in the whole book concerns the ambivalence of Huck's feelings towards Jim. At the end of Chapter 15 when Huck has played his cruel joke on Jim about the myth of their parting in the fog he feels compelled to make some gesture of reconciliation and says: 'It was fifteen minutes before I could work myself up to go and humble myself to a nigger – but I done it . . .'

Out of these and similar encounters it is the Negro who grows in stature and character rather than the guilt-ridden Huck. Yet the two of them share the supreme experience of utter freedom. Earlier in the tale as they lie on the raft Huck says, 'Jim, this is nice. I wouldn't want to be nowhere else but here. Pass me along another hunk of fish and some hot corn-bread.'

The final irony of the story, of course, is found in the fact that Jim is virtually free in life as in law. Tom makes everything clear in his almost delirious confession:

'Old Miss Watson died two months ago, and she was ashamed she ever was going to sell him down the river, and *said* so; and she set him free in her will.'

'Then what on earth did *you* want to set him free for, seeing he was already free?'

To which Tom's only answer is that he wanted the adventure of it.

Folklore and superstition

The author himself tells us that all the superstitions touched on in the book were prevalent among children and slaves in the West at the period of the story, thirty years from the date of writing.

Huckleberry Finn has a convinced belief in all the remedies that folklore provided and listens intently to each of the claims Jim makes, whether it be for the prophetic qualities of a hairball or the good fortune of being blessed with a hairy chest.

Here also the author casts a glance back to his youth. From the world of finance and the wealthy intellectuals of Connecticut, he remembered the rituals of his childhood, rituals that we have all indulged in, to ward off the powers of darkness.

In the book, however, he suggests that only white 'trash' like Pap and the simple-minded Negroes believed such nonsense. In fact all the tales were well known to the white community, and one was of white origin. The seeking out of a drowned corpse by a loaf containing a pellet of quicksilver is a piece of white-magic. An identical belief is quoted from a region on the other side of the Mississippi in the state of Illinois.

Somehow the whole idea of superstition, the themes of his boyhood and the tales of the slaves became mingled in his mind so that the author himself found it difficult to disentangle them. What he manages to do, however, is to present us with a comprehensive catalogue of most of the magic of childhood charms, potions and antidotes.

The characters

Huck's father – 'Pap'

We learn that Mark Twain took this rascal, name and all, from the local drunk who lived with the pigs, as did Huck's father. In a town full of eccentric characters Jimmy Finn had the almost-official title of town drunkard.

The author says of him elsewhere:

'He was a monument of rags and dirt: he was the profanest man in town: he had bleary eyes and a nose like a mildewed cauliflower; he slept with the hogs in an abandoned tanyard.'

Perhaps, indeed, the character has even softened in its transfer to fiction.

As the story is told through young Huck, it can, of course, only be told by impressions appropriate to a boy. Adult characters, therefore, carry extra weight as Huck is able to report their sayings and opinions without necessarily agreeing with them, or even understanding them. Pap is a useful vehicle for such ideas and prejudices. We have a good example of this in Chapter 6 when he gives vent to his feelings about the education of Negroes and the dangers attached thereto.

The totally negative part that he plays as a parent in Huck's upbringing is also of importance to the plot. It strengthens the bond between Huck and Jim, and it is not too fanciful to say that the Negro is the father the boy has always been seeking. This gives added poignancy to the way in which Jim protects Huck from the sight of his father's body in the floating frame-house early in their drift down the river. With his early dismissal from the story it would seem that Mark Twain also found him too unsavoury a character to develop fully, though he does get a sharp dig in at the do-gooders who signally fail to convert the reprobate and wholly unrepentant Pap.

Jim

'In my school days I had no aversion to slavery. I was not aware that there was anything wrong with it. No one arraigned it in my hearing ... the local pulpit taught us that God approved it, that it was a holy thing.' Mark Twain.

It was little wonder then that when he began to write the novel the author had very much in mind the typical Negro slave of the region, riddled with superstition and totally subservient to his white owner. As we have suggested earlier, Jim is much more than the rather comic-pathetic creature of fiction. At the end of the novel he has as much dignity as Mark Twain dared to give him, writing as he was in a climate antipathetic to the coloured man.

The escaped slave is Huck's protector throughout the voyage and it is his commonsense that saves the boy from danger, though the impression may appear to be quite the contrary. T. S. Eliot emphasizes the loneliness of Huckleberry Finn. Jim helps relieve this loneliness and whenever the two part their reunion is described in an almost poetic way, so closely are their destinies entwined. When Huck meets Jim again on Jackson's Island, early in the book, he is pleased that he will be able to share his lonesomeness, though his conscience does trouble him for not denouncing the escaped slave. It is difficult for the boy to see him as other than someone's property and the awakening does not come until they meet again after the parting from the raft in the fog. Then at last Huck realizes that Jim is a creature with feelings and is rightly contrite for his shabby treatment of such a friend.

Having reached this peak of understanding and gone as far as he dared in exploring the relationship between the two the author reverts to the conventional pattern at the end of the book. The manacled Jim is, once more, the bewildered Negro of fact and fiction and it is only the timely intervention of the doctor that prevents the accepted treatment for such offences as he has committed – lynching.

Tom Sawyer

The guiding spirit of the novel that bears his name has a lesser part in *Huckleberry Finn*, but a vital one nonetheless. He is the genius under whose influence Huckleberry Finn 'stands rebuked'. Tom has the imagination, Huck the sense to see through him. Yet he still envies Tom the finish that would add the touch of the master to his own poor efforts to deal with the situations he finds himself in. Early in the book he says:

'I did wish Tom Sawyer was there, I knowed he would take an interest in this kind of business, and throw in the fancy touches. Nobody could spread himself like Tom Sawyer in such a thing as that.'

This about his efforts to cover his tracks as he escapes from the Island.

Of their decision to board the *Walter Scott* he says:

'Do you reckon Tom Sawyer would ever go by this thing? Not for pie he wouldn't. He'd call it an adventure.'

As the novel develops and the character of Huck grows with it we find him getting closer to the attitude of his hero and being less self-effacing in his claims. In Chapter 28 he congratulates himself on the handling of the Mary Jane episode and the story of the virulent mumps she has gone to nurse.

I reckoned Tom Sawyer couldn't a' done it no neater himself. Of course he would a' throwed more style into it, but I can't do that very handy, not being brung up to it.

So, until he appears again at the end of the novel we glean our knowledge of Tom through the comments of Huck. When he does enter the plot he wants to know everything.

And he wanted to know all about it right off; because it was a grand adventure, and mysterious, and so it hit him where he lived.

For a while it would almost seem that the servant had managed to outdo the master. But not for long:

Tom had his store clothes on, and an audience – and that was always nuts for Tom Sawyer.

Soon he is in his old place as leader and organizer:

... And Tom superintended. He could out superintend any boy I ever see. He knowed how to do everything.

When Tom appears, Huck reverts to his subsidiary role and he even submits to what Tom finds amusing although it actually prolongs the suffering of the unfortunate Negro. The protracted ending of the story that so many critics have commented on can be laid wholly to the charge of Tom. Here is elaboration on elaboration, and jape piled on jape until we feel overwhelmed by the enormity of the whole plot that seems to have taken over completely. Tom, like Frankenstein, has created something that he can no longer control. It should be noted, however, that the author takes every opportunity in the situation that can give him an opening to poke fun at generations of romantic and historical novelists. We are bewildered by the catalogue of 'tricks' used by these vastly popular writers and the author leaves them little new to add to their repertoire.

Huckleberry Finn

As we have already suggested, the first of the two adventure novels, *Tom Sawyer*, is narrated more or less from Tom's point of view. In the second, Mark Twain commits himself almost wholly to the view of Huckleberry Finn. It is only when some rather deeper adult concept of morality is touched on that the author uses an adult to suggest it, and Huck to pass it on to the reader as though we couldn't really expect him to follow the logic of this alien world of the grown-up.

The hero of this novel bears a heavy load on young and untutored shoulders. His opinions are spontaneous, but generally, despite his lack of years and experience, correct. He has an almost total sympathy with his fellow man no matter how bad he may appear on the surface. If he writes about rogues the author chooses superlative rogues, rather after the manner of Chaucer who saw the same kind of good in unsavoury characters like the Pardoner. This sympathy is passed on to Huck in no small measure.

Linked with his sympathy, however, is a king-sized conscience which troubles Huck through the book, and, indeed, beyond. After the manner of most of us he knows what is right, but frequently finds that he is unable to do it for some reason not of his own contriving. Despite all his bravado there is a healthy respect for the law lurking not too far beneath the surface. The old morality of rewards and punishments is the standard by which he lives. At times the boy is our conscience as we follow his thinking; at others he acts as Chorus to events, chronicling them as an impassive observer caught in a situation that he cannot be held responsible for and is unable to control.

If the novel is basically about the freedom of the individual, then it is about Huck's freedom. At the start of the book he is hedged around by convention and the laws of polite society. These are irksome to the majority of us so we share something of Huck's exultation as he escapes both physically and spiritually from these restraints. The river gives him a physical barrier from his fellows and his periods of solitariness on the raft give him a near mystical understanding of the universe. This almost natural boy is very close indeed to the nature that surrounds him.

The author, however, is not completely prepared to leave the boy to his own devices at the end of the novel. Although Huck says:

I reckon I got to light out for the Territory ahead of the rest, because Aunt Sally she's going to adopt me and civilize me, and I can't stand it. I been there before.

we feel that civilization will gather him in again.

Notes

Link with the end of *Tom Sawyer*:

So endeth this chronicle. It being strictly the history of a boy, it must stop here; the story could not go much further without becoming the history of a man.

When one writes a novel about grown people, he [sic] knows exactly where to stop – that is, with a marriage; but when he writes of juveniles, he must stop where he best can.

Most of the characters that perform in this book still live, and are prosperous and happy. Some day it may seem worth while to take up the story of the young ones again, and see what sort of men and women they turned out to be; therefore it will be wisest not to reveal any of that part of their lives at present.

Chapter 1

We are introduced to our hero, Huckleberry Finn, after he has shared the 12,000-dollar reward with Tom Sawyer. He is none too happy with his adopted mother, the widow Douglas, and is already chafing under the restraints of being 'civilized'. The old meeting call of Tom Sawyer has him shinning down the shed roof and off to freedom.

sugar-hogshead large barrel used for carrying sugar.
nigger the ordinary term used for a slave, not necessarily abusive.

Chapter 2

The first of the practical jokes played on Jim, Miss Watson's Negro servant. While he is asleep under a tree, the boys hang his hat from a branch to make him believe that the witches have placed it there. He capitalizes on the story and adds details until it grows far out of proportion to the facts.

Tom Sawyer's band of robbers is formed. Instead of killing their victims, they decide to compromise on ransom, though they are not too clear as to what that will entail.

Huck returns to his room with his new clothes in the state to which he has been most accustomed: 'greased up and clayey'.

we looked down into the village Hannibal, Missouri; other
frontier towns featured in the book are virtually descriptions of
Hannibal.
how in the nation polite term for 'how in damnation'.

Chapter 3

The consequences of the previous night's escapade are not too serious.

Huck's father has not been seen for over a year; this suits Huck, but he does not accept the suggestion that his father is the man found drowned.

Tom Sawyer's imagination over the robbing of the picnic party is not enough to hold the loyalty of his followers. Tom tells Huckleberry how magicians call up genies by rubbing lamps; Huckleberry's private experiment with an old lamp fails to call up any 'genies' and he remains sceptical.

sumter mules pack animals.
ambuscade ambush.
primer kindergarten or primary class.
Don Quixote 17th-century tale by the Spanish author Cervantes.
genies guardian spirits ready at the call of their masters to do
anything asked of them.

Chapter 4

A gap of three or four months. An unfortunate incident with a spilled salt-cellar, and the mark in the snow of a hob-nailed boot with the sign of the cross in it, has Huck racing for Judge Thatcher. He signs over his fortune of 6,000 dollars to the judge, and consults the 'hair-ball' of the Negro slave Jim for news of 'Pap'.

A completely equivocal reading of Huck's future is capped by the boy returning to his room to find his father installed there.

hookey truant.
hair-ball formed by the animal licking its fur; thought to have soothsaying properties.

Chapter 5

Huck confronts Pap, who chides him over his new-found wealth and status. The boy placates him with the one dollar he has left as receipt for his bargain with the judge. This is enough for Pap to buy whisky and to demand custody of his son. A new circuit-judge, ignorant of the facts and on humanitarian grounds, leaves Huck with his father. The judge's philanthropy is sorely tried when the repentant sinner returns to his drunken ways after a very short reformation.

sass cheek; our 'sauce'.
I'll make him pungle pay, or give up. That is why, in Chapter 4, as soon as Huck saw his father's footprints he made a token transfer of his wealth to Judge Thatcher.
jug of forty-rod strong enough to knock a man that distance.

Chapter 6

Pap kidnaps his son and they camp on the Illinois side of the river. A stolen gun ensures their privacy. In a perverse way, Huck enjoys the 'freedom' of his new life, restricted though it is.

In his father's absence from the hut, Huck finds a rusty saw and by working on the main bottom log manages to provide himself with an escape route should he need it.

Huck's father rages fiercely against a government that gives a Negro slave education and, final betrayal, the vote. An attack of the DTs transforms Pap into a raving lunatic, determined to kill Huck, now the 'Angel of Death'. After fury – rest, and Huck arms himself with the gun ready to face his father on his awakening.

two newspapers for wadding used to pack the load of guns at that period.
tow shredded flax.
mulatter mulatto; half-breed.
delirium tremens hallucinations brought on by heavy drinking; the kind of bout that Pap suffers in this chapter.
split-bottom splint-bottom.

Chapter 7

Pap, when he does wake up, obviously has no memory of his previous behaviour and leaves the boy. Huck finds a drifting canoe brought down the river by the June tide, and he hides it in a creek for future use. While his father is off to town to sell drift-logs, Huck prepares the craft with necessary provisions.

He covers his tracks and gives the impression that the cabin has been attacked and he himself dragged off and dumped in the river.

He picks on Jackson's Island as his place of concealment. Pap's return speeds Huck's departure, and he takes particular care when passing the ferry-landing.

trot-line one fishing line with various others hooked and stemming from it.
dipper cup-like container with a long straight handle used for dipping into liquids.

gourd flask.

whetstone a stone used for sharpening cutlery, etc., by friction.

Jackson's Island also used in *Tom Sawyer*; actually Glassock's Island, since eroded by the Mississippi.

Chapter 8

Huck hears the sound of the cannon fired to raise the bodies of the drowned. He eagerly gathers the 'quicksilver' loaves as manna from heaven. The ferryboat with his friends aboard is brought close enough ashore for Huck to distinguish them all.

Three days and nights of total isolation and freedom are shattered by the discovery of a still-warm camp fire.

He determines to find out who his fellow-settlers are and finds the escaped slave, Jim. They while away the time with folk-tales and Negro lore.

firing cannon over the water It was thought that the vibration caused would dislodge a drowned body.

quicksilver mercury. This is the only example of 'white-magic' in the book.

corn-pone rough corn-bread baked of maize.

camp-fire still smoking As dramatic a discovery as the footprint found by Robinson Crusoe.

low-down Abolitionist Those who were against slavery in the USA.

Illinois Legally free soil for the escaping slaves.

bank too bluff too steep.

plug er dog-leg cheap tobacco.

wood-flat flat-bottomed boat for carrying timber.

Chapter 9

Exploration of the cave. Ten or twelve days of high winds and rain bring floods. A whole frame-house floats down river and they paddle out and clamber aboard this strange craft. The body of a man, shot in some gambling argument, lies dead in a corner, and Jim warns Huck not to look at his face – 'it's too gashly'. They help themselves to some necessary trifles and return to the Island.

lumber raft for carrying timber.
it might come good turn out to be useful.
Barlow knife one-bladed jack-knife named after the maker.
reticule small purse or bag.
currycomb a comb, usually with rows of metal teeth, used for cleaning horses.

Chapter 10

A practical joke misfires. Huck puts a dead rattlesnake in Jim's bed and its mate, coming to seek it, bites the Negro. Pap's whisky is used as an antidote and it is difficult to tell whether that or the poison causes Jim's delirium.

A tall fishing story of the man-sized catfish.

Huck disguises himself as a girl, using the clothes found in the floating house, and makes his way to the mainland in search of news.

Chapter 11

Huck takes on the identity of Sarah Williams, and the woman he meets tells him the local gossip about his own disappearance and supposed murder. Opinion seems to vary between Huck's father and Jim as the murderer. The woman mentions her desire for the 300-dollar reward for Jim's capture and also the fact that she has seen smoke on Jackson's Island.

Huck makes three mistakes, apart from forgetting his assumed name, that show the woman she is entertaining a boy rather than a girl: the needle-threading, the throwing of the lead weight at the rats, and the instinctive closing of the legs to catch the lead rather than the making of a lap. Huck spins another tale to account for his disguise.

The woman has convinced Huck of the danger to Jim by her interest in the Negro, and Huck swiftly returns to the island with the determination that they must move at once.

runaway 'prentice an apprentice who has run off before serving his time.
St Petersburg Hannibal.

Chapter 12

Huck and Jim prepare the raft for a long voyage down river. They spot a steamboat marooned on the rocks and decide to board her. They witness a strange incident in the state-room with one man, Jim Turner, being threatened by two other men called Jake Packard and Bill. Huck and Jim decide it is time to leave, but their raft has drifted away.

cottonwood American poplars; cottonlike tufts on seeds.
p'simmons persimmons: trees bearing astringent plumlike fruit that is sweet and edible when ripe.
texas officers' cabin. All the state-rooms were called after the American states, and this was the largest – hence the name.
labboard port, or left side.
guys ropes for hoisting or dropping cargo.
crawfished crawled backwards.

Chapter 13

Huck and Jim make their getaway in the boat Packard and Bill have tied alongside the hulk. By good luck they chance on their raft floating ahead of them. Huck spins a yarn to the watchman at the next village about his family being aboard the wreck – the *Walter Scott* at Booth's Landing, as it turns out.

The rescue attempt is too late, but Huck feels content that the widow Douglas would have been glad that he had at least tried to help the miscreants.

bitts posts set in pairs on decks for fastening cables.

Chapter 14

Huck regales Jim with tales of royalty and the ease with which such fortunates go through life. The Negro totally misunderstands the point of the King-Solomon-and-the-baby story – or does he? Their conversation proceeds to linguistic problems and the matter of communication between the races. Huck's determined logic passes completely over Jim's head and the argument is abandoned.

Sollermun Solomon: see Kings I. iii, 16–27.
Louis XVI and the dolphin The Dauphin, Louis Charles, who survived the execution of his father, Louis XVI, in 1793, and died in prison.

Chapter 15

They encounter fog for the first time, and canoe and raft are parted. After various vicissitudes Huck catches up with Jim and the raft and starts an elaborate masquerade about their never having been parted in any fog. Jim, in his turn, starts on an interpretation of the so-called dream. The reality of the leaves and rubbish and the broken oar pierces the cruelty of Huck's jape, and Jim, in deeply moving fashion, shows his real concern for the boy and his fear that he had genuinely come to grief and been lost.

Cairo pronounced 'Kay-ro'.

sell the raft and get on a steamboat and go way up the Ohio amongst the free States Mark Twain left the book aside near the end of Chapter 16 and instead of proceeding with Jim's attempt to freedom became enthralled with the idea of the River and its peculiar freedom.

staving dream fine, splendid dream.

Chapter 16

The thought of freedom ahead for Jim as they approach Cairo troubles Huck's conscience. Faced with an opportunity of betraying the Negro, Huck draws back at the last moment and puts off two enquirers with tales of smallpox aboard the raft. For his story, and in order to protect themselves from the disease, the enquirers float forty dollars to him on a board – real wealth for Huck and Jim. By a rapid reversal of fortune, they are struck head-on by a paddle-steamer and abandon their raft. Huck loses sight of Jim, but manages to make a safe landing; he comes across a house.

long sweeps long oar to propel or steer a raft.

looard to the lee side; the side to which the wind blows; opposite to windward.

outside was the old regular Muddy Cairo lies at the point where the Ohio and the Mississipi rivers flow together; they know they have passed the town in the fog when they see the clear water from the Ohio still flowing along the East bank of the Mississippi.

towards the left-hand shore Kentucky, where the feud that follows takes place.

Chapter 17

Huck changes his identity yet again, this time to 'George Jackson', when challenged from the house. When he satisfies the Grangerfords that he is not of the Shepherdson family, with whom the Grangerfords are feuding, he is welcomed into their home. The lazy mode of life of his new kinsfolk is immediately to Huck's liking. He spends some time enumerating the artistic and literary achievements of Emmeline Grangerford, gifted and precocious daughter of the family, who had not lived long enough to fulfil her early promise.

roundabout short, close-fitting jacket.
Friendship's Offering Collection of poetry and prose designed as a gift book.
Ode to Stephen Dowling Bots, Dec'd Parody of the gloomy popular poetry of the time.

Chapter 18

Huck describes Colonel Grangerford and the deference accorded him and his wife by the rest of the family. He witnesses a brush with a Shepherdson, and learns that the original cause of the feud has been clouded by the passing of some thirty years. He stumbles on the Romeo and Juliet situation of Miss Sophia and one of the Shepherdsons.

The Negro servant of the house takes Huck to the swamp, and once more he is reunited with Jim. The raft, after all, had not been destroyed.

There is great consternation at the house when it is discovered that Sophia has run off with Harvey Shepherdson. Huck is sickened by the whole business of the feud, and haunted by the waste of life, particularly that of Buck, the young Grangerford, who had been so good to him. Huck and Jim make another rapid escape on the raft.

mudcat less esteemed variety of catfish.
preforeordestination Comic mingling of two religious tenets, predestination and foreordination.
coarse-hand printing.

Chapter 19

A journey ashore brings to Huck and Jim aboard their raft the doubtful company of two charlatans. The younger man claims to be a descendant of the Duke of Bridgewater, and the elder, elaborating on the joke, claims to be the Dauphin (and 'late' at that!) of France.

Jim is overawed by the presence of such royalty, but Huck is less impressed, though prepared to go along with their game for the sake of peace and quiet.

a chute a narrow channel to the mainland with fast-flowing water.
jour printer journeyman printer: not yet a master printer.
What's your lay? What is your job? The travelling fraud was a stock character in the literature of the time.
at your age Had the Dauphin lived he would have been in his mid-fifties.

Chapter 20

The two new arrivals are suspicious about Jim being a runaway slave, but Huck, with another elaborate story, allays their fears. With plans to present a Shakespearian production, the four of them go ashore, to find the local community held fast by a Revival Meeting. The 'King', loath to let an opportunity of displaying his histrionic talent go by, becomes the star turn at the Penitents' Bench, and has a handsome collection for reward.

The 'Duke', on the other hand, has not been idle in the printing office, and besides gaining some advances on subscriptions has printed a cover-poster for Jim, so that it would seem that they were taking him in chains to his rightful punishment if anyone became too inquisitive.

Garrick the Younger non-existent actor.
Juliet The audience would be more upset by the King's age than by his sex.

work that camp meeting for all it was worth A stock
  situation of frontier humour was the pious fraud who made off
  with the collection.

Chapter 21

After the revels of the previous night, the Duke and the King
make a late appearance. Rehearsals are soon under way for
the projected performance with a finely muddled soliloquy,
allegedly spoken by Hamlet, being prepared for any encore
that may be requested.

  The posters are soon displayed in the small town, but the
arrival of one Boggs – 'in from the country for his little old
monthly drunk' – holds attention for a while. He is vilifying
a Colonel Sherburn, who, for very little reason, puts an end
to the abuse by shooting Boggs dead. The crowd rouses itself
to a fury against the Colonel, and bays for a lynching.

Capet When Louis XVI was convicted, the National Convention
  used his family name, Louis Capet. Here, it is a possible
  garbling of Capulet, Juliet's family name.
speech from Shakespeare a muddling of some of the
  playwright's most memorable lines.
show-bill Another muddle of famous Shakespearian actors.

Chapter 22

Sherburn faces the crowd and lashes them with his tongue
for the cowards that he knows them to be.

  As light relief to the previous tension, Huck enjoys a visit
to the Circus. In contrast to that audience, the handful that
turn out to watch the King and Duke seems an insult to them;
psychological tactics are resorted to for the next performance
which is for male eyes only.

Chapter 23

The performance of 'The Royal Nonesuch' – the anti-climax of the King's appearance as a naked zebra. Once more, psychology is used to prevent the audience becoming a laughing-stock to the rest of the townsfolk. They determine to keep the nature of the performance secret.

Huck and Jim consider the idiosyncrasies of kingship. Jim is fast becoming disillusioned by the breed. He reminisces about his family ties and tells of his shock on discovering that his daughter was deaf.

Henry VIII A great mixture of history and fiction.

Chapter 24

Another trick to save Jim having to hide in the wigwam on the raft every day. He is made up as a peepshow – a 'sick Arab' – with a sign round his neck suggesting he is not quite sane. The King runs into the saga of the Wilks family, willingly unfolded by a young man waiting for the steamboat. Now the King sets himself out to be the brother from England, with the Duke cast in the role of the deaf-mute brother.

Chapter 25

News of their arrival spreads fast, and the bereaved family greets the impostors eagerly. They are soon firmly ensconced, inviting friends of the deceased to share supper with them. The Will is read and the 6,000 dollars in cash soon found in the cellar. The King and the Duke are so pleased with their haul that they make up the 415 dollars deficit out of their theatrical takings. They present the girls with the cash, a step calculated to allay any suspicions of their honesty. The King explains away his malapropism of funeral 'orgies' instead of 'obsequies' at least to his own satisfaction; the Doctor, however, refuses to be taken in by the patent fraud and will not accept this 'Harvey Wilks' as Peter's brother. When the scene reaches direct confrontation, Mary Jane thrusts the money into the King's hands as proof of her acceptance of his identity. Foiled for the moment, the Doctor makes his exit.

The Wilks episode Up to now, the jokes have been at a harmless level; now they descend to the exploitation of a grief-stricken family.

doxolojer the Doxology. Praise God from whom all blessings flow.

Chapter 26

The hare-lipped sister, Joanna, begins to ask Huck questions about London that he finds too close for comfort. Gradually, however, he is captivated by the girls' honesty, and determines that he will not see them cheated. Hiding behind a curtain, Huck hears the two rogues plotting to sell the house before making their escape with the cash. A new hiding place for the latter, in the straw ticking under the feather-bed, gives Huck his opportunity, and soon he is off with it to his own room.

pallet straw mattress.

congress water mineral water from Congress Springs at Saratoga, New York.

Chapter 27

Huck hits on a macabre hiding place for the cash – in the coffin. There follows a cameo picture of the perfect under-taker ready for any eventuality, even quietening a dog chasing a rat in the basement.

After the burial, Huck is still bewildered as to whether the money has been discovered or not.

The King makes a tactical error when selling the slaves in splitting a Negro family. He and the Duke discover the money is missing, and question Huck, who lays the blame for the theft at the Negroes' door. The two plotters blame themselves for their lack of vigilance and are concerned that the draft for the sale of the niggers has been lodged in the bank for subsequent collection.

Chapter 28

Huck unfolds the whole story to Mary Jane, and advises her to leave town for several days. He intends to use '*Royal Nonesuch, Bricksville*' in the last resort for identification of the two frauds.

Huck spins a tale to the two other sisters of a virulent kind of mumps that Mary Jane has gone to nurse. They are none too eager to spread the news to their 'Uncle Harvey' lest their trip to Europe be postponed.

The sale goes well until another Harvey Wilks turns up, – and stand up the real heir to Peter Wilks's fortune!

Chapter 29

The contest between the real and the sham. The lawyer, Levi Bell, tells the crowd that he saw Huck and the King at the Point in a canoe.

The writing test is a failure as proof of identity, but birthmarks are more of a problem. Argument wages over what the deceased had tattooed on his breast. Exhumation appears to be the only solution, and they repair to the graveyard. Instead of any sign of identification, the bag of gold is discovered in the coffin and Huck makes off rapidly. An opportune canoe takes him swiftly to the raft and Jim, but, unhappily, they have not yet rid themselves of the King and the Duke.

Chapter 30

Angry recriminations follow. The thieves fall out about who actually hid the gold in the coffin. They seek consolation in the bottle and are soon comrades again, even after the King, under duress, has falsely confessed to being the one who hid the gold.

Chapter 31

The two rogues try a variety of tricks to raise money, from temperance meetings to elocution. There is some mischief brewing which Huck cannot fathom, but he has his suspicions on returning to the raft to find that Jim has disappeared. The King has betrayed him for forty dollars.

Huck's conscience troubles him about his next move. He tears up the letter he was about to send to Miss Watson, and decides that he will risk damnation rather than betray Jim. Another run-in with the Duke confirms Huck's fears about the Negro. The Duke deliberately misleads Huck as to Jim's new owner, but after talking to a local boy, Huck already has it in mind to visit the Phelps' household.

a little low doggery grog-shop or low type of saloon.

Chapter 32

Huck's arrival at the Phelps' farm is greeted by a pack of barking dogs, but they turn out more friendly than they first appear.

Huck cheerfully accepts his new role as 'cousin Tom', whoever he may be. The timely subterfuge of Aunt Sally gives Huck and the reader the shock of discovering that the Tom referred to is none other than Tom Sawyer. The only fear now is that the real Tom will give the game away as his arrival is obviously due at any moment. In the hope of waylaying Tom, Huck tells the family that he will go to the town to fetch his luggage.

one-horse cotton plantations like the farm of Twain's uncle, John Quarles, near Hannibal.

Chapter 33

Huck meets Tom on the way to town; to Tom, Huck is as though risen from the grave, but Huck soon explains all his circumstances. The crucial point of their meeting comes when Huck tells of his plans to steal Jim. Tom agrees to help, and in a perverted way loses face with Huck for so doing. They agree to separate so that Tom can make his individual arrival. True to his nature, this has to be dramatic, and he surprises Aunt Sally by his boldness in kissing her on the mouth. All is well when he makes clear his new identity – Sid Sawyer.

The two boys wait to hear news of Jim. When one of the children asks if they may go to see the show that evening, Uncle Silas says that the 'runaway nigger' revealed details of that scandalous show, and the performers will probably be driven out of town. Huck decides to try and warn them, and he and Tom sneak out of their room later; they see the King and the Duke, tarred and feathered, being run out of town. Even at this point Huck shows no animosity and has pity in his heart for the pair of them.

Chapter 34

They discover Jim's prison. An over-simplified plan of escape does not appeal to the ingenious mind of Tom Sawyer. He

scorns the simple wrenching away of a board from a window
and the immediate release of the prisoner. An adjoining shed
suggests a tunnel as access route to the prisoner and the chance
of a week's hard work ahead.

Once more Huck and Jim are reunited by the simple method
of following the Negro who carries the prisoner's food.

Chapter 35

Elaborate plans are made for a 'proper' escape to be
organized. A mixture of fiction and history is called to their
aid for the attempt to be authentic. All the wiles of a Château
d'If (of *The Count of Monte Cristo* fame) operation, including
a journal kept by the prisoner and written in his own blood,
are to be used. Any short-cuts suggested by Huck are greeted
with the scorn they deserve.

fox-fire phosphorescent glow from decaying wood.
Baron Trenck etc All these made daring attempted or successful
  escapes.
The Iron Mask Hero of Alexandre Dumas's novel, Vicomte de
  Bragelonne, the mysterious masked prisoner who died unknown
  in the Bastille in 1703.

Chapter 36

The length of the task of digging out the dirt foundations
under the hut, and the blisters on his hands, force Tom to
compromise and use ordinary pick and shovel while pretend-
ing they are case-knives. Plans are made with Jim as to how
he is to receive the tools necessary for his escape – Nat, the
nigger servant, and Uncle Silas are to be the unwitting
carriers. The advent of some eleven of the farm dogs into the
shed (the boys having left the lean-to shed open) almost gives
the whole show away. A witch-pie is suggested as a remedy

for supernatural happenings and accepted by the over-gullible Nat.

Chapter 37

The boys collect the ingredients for the infamous pie – surely the finest baking ever received by any prisoner!

Aunt Sally becomes a trifle suspicious at the loss of Uncle Silas's second shirt from the line. Other mysterious losses from her cutlery also concern her, as well as six candles going missing. A crazy game of the disappearing spoon, organized by Tom, soon rids them of any fear of a serious count. The baking causes some trouble, the sheet-rope seeming to be endless and the capacity of the pie too slight for its concealment. At last the whole thing is safely delivered.

Chapter 38

They set to as pen makers, but Tom finds the designing of a coat-of-arms more to his taste, as was the composition of 'mournful inscriptions' to be found in the prison after the bird had flown. A pet for the prisoner is the next item on the agenda; even a rattlesnake is acceptable – but not to Jim! A flower, watered by the prisoner's tears, causes difficulty as Jim, apparently, rarely cries. The ever-resourceful Tom suggests an onion as a final remedy to make the tears flow.

Chapter 39

Rats and snakes collected for the prisoner's comfort cause embarrassment by their refusal to stay captive. The boys are held responsible for the plague of snakes and beaten soundly whenever one appears. Jim finds his unwholesome companions more of a trial than a solace to his captivity. Various signs are delivered to the family giving notice of some impending disaster.

allycumpain an ointment made of oil of garlic and used by the
Indians to soothe insect bites.
Ingean Territory Oklahoma: the Indian federal land which
became a refuge for unsavoury characters.

Chapter 40

Aunt Sally discovers Huck in the cellar and the rapid con-
cealment of a lump of butter is called for – under his hat.
The subsequent melting mess is initially diagnosed by Aunt
Sally as brain fever.

The posse, alerted by Tom's anonymous warning, is already
gathered, and soon finds itself in the cabin with the would-be
escapers, neither being able to see the other in the dark. In
the ensuing mêlée Tom has the supreme satisfaction of having
a bullet in the leg. He, Huck and Jim flee to the raft. The
last part of the jigsaw is to be put in place with the
summoning of the doctor, and the plan of his being led
blindfolded to the heart of the wood and the near-dying
victim.

Chapter 41

The doctor actually makes the journey alone to where Tom
lies. Huck, by bad luck, runs right into the arms of Uncle
Silas. A visit to the Post Office, where Huck alleges 'Sid' can
be found, puts the uncle in possession of a soon-forgotten
letter.

Huck, the prodigal son, is given the appropriate welcome.
The local gossips exult over the recent happenings and give
vent to their personal emotions. The non-return of 'Sid' causes
concern. Huck, put on his honour not to leave his bedroom,
faces a cruel dilemma in his desire to search for his friend.

Chapter 42

The letter is remembered, but before it can be read the inert body of Tom is brought in on a mattress, accompanied by the doctor and Jim, his hands shackled. Things look none too healthy for the Negro, but the doctor speaks up on his behalf. Tom makes a rapid recovery from the effect of his wounds. Aunt Sally listens to the whole tale from his own lips. It transpires that Jim has already been set free by the Will of the recently deceased Miss Watson.

The sudden appearance of Aunt Polly adds further to the confusion, but eventually personalities are sorted out and the explanatory letters unearthed.

Aunt Polly Tom's relative and a leading figure in *The Adventures of Tom Sawyer*.

Chapter the last

Huck upbraids Tom for the final deceit of Jim's escape and hears the projected grand finale of the freed slave's triumphant return to his home town. Jim, at last, accepts the omen of a hairy chest as proof of his good fortune. Huck's nest-egg of 6,000 dollars proves to have been untouched and there will be no more trouble from Pap – his was the body in the house floating down the river.

So the last piece is fixed in the jigsaw, and we leave Huck, the wheel having come full circle, faced with the unwelcome prospect of being civilized again.

Revision questions

1 What do you consider, from your reading of the novel, to be Huck's attitude towards being civilized?

2 What part do nature and scenery take in the novel?

3 Consider this book as a study of loneliness.

4 'The River is as important as the characters in the novel.' Discuss.

5 What attitude does the author take towards the problem of slavery? Give incidents from the text.

6 'Prejudice of whatever kind is hateful to Mark Twain.' Discuss.

7 'Tom Sawyer eventually ousts Huck Finn as the hero of the novel.' Do you agree?

8 Consider at least three of the American traditions that Mark Twain satirizes in this novel.

9 Write a character sketch of Huck's father.

10 'There are too many coincidences in the novel for it to ring true.' Do you agree?

11 Write an essay on superstition and folklore as they appear in this book.

12 What is the author's attitude towards royalty as you find it in the novel?

13 'Mark Twain is a master of dialect and colloquial speech.' Discuss.

14 Show that the author was a superb judge of character from your reading of the book.

15 What is the function of the Negro, Jim, in the book?

16 Give examples of the author's ability to recall scenes of his boyhood.

17 'The author is steeped in romantic fiction.' Choose some examples from the text in support of this statement.

18 'The end of the book is tedious and contrived.' Discuss.

19 Would you consider this to be the really great American novel?

20 'From first to last a river pilot.' Consider this estimate of Mark Twain from your reading of *Huckleberry Finn*.

Student's notes

Student's notes